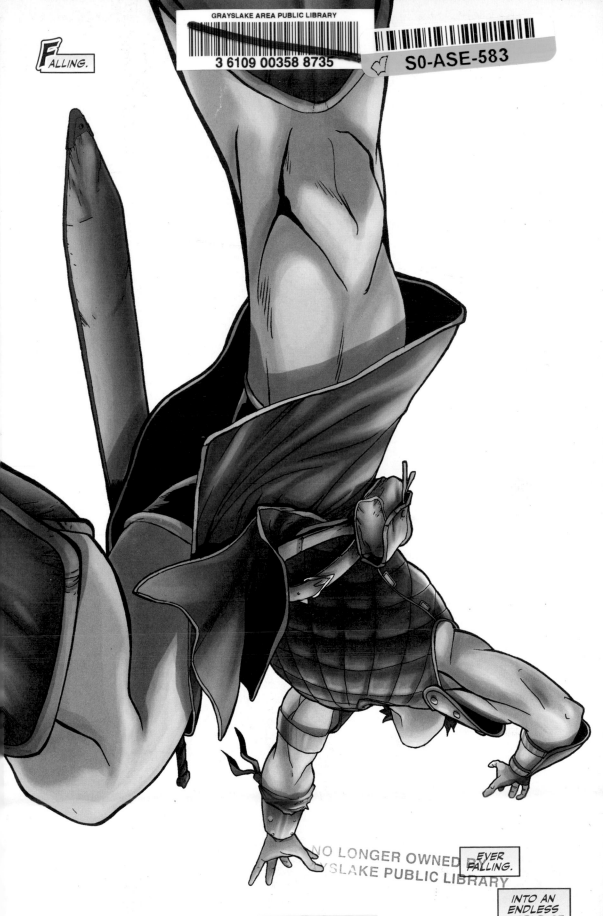

HAD IT BEEN
SECONDS?
HOURS? DAYS?

ONE MINUTE,
BILLOS WAS IN
THE FOREST.

WAS HE
DEAD?
ALIVE?

THE NEXT, HE
FOUND HIMSELF
IN THIS --

THERE WAS
NO WAY TO
TELL.

-- NOTHINGNESS.

SOME STATE
IN-BETWEEN?

WHETHER THIS WAS OF ELYON'S MAKING --

ANOTHER THING HAD BECOME ALL TOO CLEAR TO BILLOS.

HE WAS UTTERLY --

ENTIRELY --

-- ALONE.

-- OR OF TEELEH, ONE THING WAS CERTAIN --

-- HE WAS GOING MAD -- OR, PERHAPS, ALREADY WAS.

PAINFULLY --

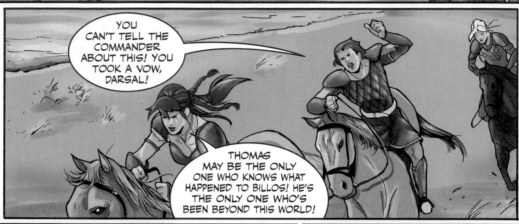

OWWW!

LET GO, JOHNIS!

I'M SERIOUS, YOU BRAT.

OOOOF!

SPLASHH

WITH OR WITHOUT YOU, I'M GOING TO FIND BILLOS!

IF THAT MEANS GOING TO THE COMMANDER AND SPOILING OUR SECRET LITTLE MISSION --

-- SO BE IT.

KA-SPLASSSHH

WHAT WHAT DOES THAT HAVE TO DO WITH BILLOS?

BILLOS --

BILLOS WAS TALKING ABOUT YOUR -- *DREAMWORLD* -- BEFORE HE WENT MISSING.

IT WASN'T SO LONG AGO THAT I COULD BREATHE ELYON'S WATER.

DO YOU BELIEVE THAT?

YES.

AND DO YOU BELIEVE THE REST OF IT?

THAT THERE WAS ONCE NO DISEASE? THAT ROUSH ONCE PROTECTED US FROM THE EVIL SHATAIKI? THAT ELYON HIMSELF ONCE LIVED AMONG US?

YES.

THEN YOU ARE WISER THAN MANY WHO HAVE LOST THEIR FAITH IN THE UNSEEN.

STILL, YOU MAY FIND WHAT I'M ABOUT TO TELL YOU EVEN HARDER TO BELIEVE.

THE TRUTH IS -- I HAVE BEEN BEYOND THIS WORLD*.

*READ THE CIRCLE TRILOGY (BLACK, RED AND WHITE) GRAPHIC NOVELS FOR THE FULL STORY.

IN FACT, THERE ARE PEOPLE WHO WOULD SWEAR TO YOU THAT I'M LIVING IN THE HISTORIES, SLEEPING IN A PLACE CALLED BANGKOK AT THIS VERY MOMENT.

THOSE SAME PEOPLE WOULD TELL YOU I'VE ONLY SLEPT FOR HOURS IN THAT REALITY, DREAMING OF THE LAST THIRTEEN YEARS HERE.

YOU, ON THE OTHER HAND, MIGHT TELL ME THESE VISIONS OF BANGKOK ARE ONLY A DREAM. BUT WHICH REALITY IS REAL?

BOTH.

THAT'S RIGHT.

JUST BECAUSE WE CAN'T SEE BANGKOK, DOESN'T MEAN IT DOESN'T EXIST.

SO YOU'RE SAYING BILLOS COULD'VE GONE TO THIS DREAM-WORLD OF YOURS?

NOT EXACTLY.

AND IF YOU'RE EVEN THINKING OF TRYING TO GO AFTER HIM, TO CROSS THE BREACH BETWEEN WORLDS -- DON'T.

ONLY AN IDIOT WOULD SUGGEST I RISK WARRIORS TO FIND A GUARD WHO'S BEEN LOST LESS THAN AN HOUR.

NONE OF YOU ARE IDIOTS, WHICH TELLS ME YOU'RE DEFINITELY HIDING SOMETHING.

IT'S -- IT'S NOTHING, SIR.

WHAT SHE MEANS IS --

-- IT'S NOTHING TO ANYONE, BUT US.

WE'VE TAKEN A VOW NOT TO WHISPER A WORD OF IT TO ANYONE.

ELYON KNOWS WHAT'S HAPPENING HERE IS BEYOND ME. BEYOND ANY OF US.

SO TAKE THIS VERY PRIVATE, VERY PERSONAL THING AWAY FROM ME.

ONE MORE THING --

-- I WANT YOU TO STAY TOGETHER UNTIL YOU FIND BILLOS. DON'T LEAVE THE VILLAGE AND DON'T LEAVE EACH OTHER'S SIGHT. AM I CLEAR?

YES, COMMANDER.

PERFECTLY, SIR.

DARSAL?

O-OH, YES. YES, SIR.

SWEET ELYON, WHAT AM I GOING TO DO WITH THEM?

WHAT WE HAVE TO DO IS FIND ANOTHER BOOK.

ELYON GAVE US A MISSION. TO FIND THE ORIGINAL SEVEN BOOKS OF HISTORY.

FOUR, OF WHICH, ARE STILL MISSING.

ALL SEVEN ARE MISSING, IF YOU COUNT THE THREE BILLOS STOLE.

YOU ASKED US TO FOLLOW YOU TO THE END OF THE EARTH AND WE DID. YOU DEMANDED WE SPARE THE HORDE AND WE DID.

EACH TIME YOU WERE RIGHT.

NOW YOU SAY SIT AND WAIT. ARE YOU RIGHT THIS TIME?

BASED ON WHAT I KNOW --

-- YES.

YOU BETTER BE, SCRAPPER.

WHERE ARE YOU GOING?

PLEASE TELL ME WAITING DOESN'T MEAN I HAVE TO HOLD MY BLADDER TOO.

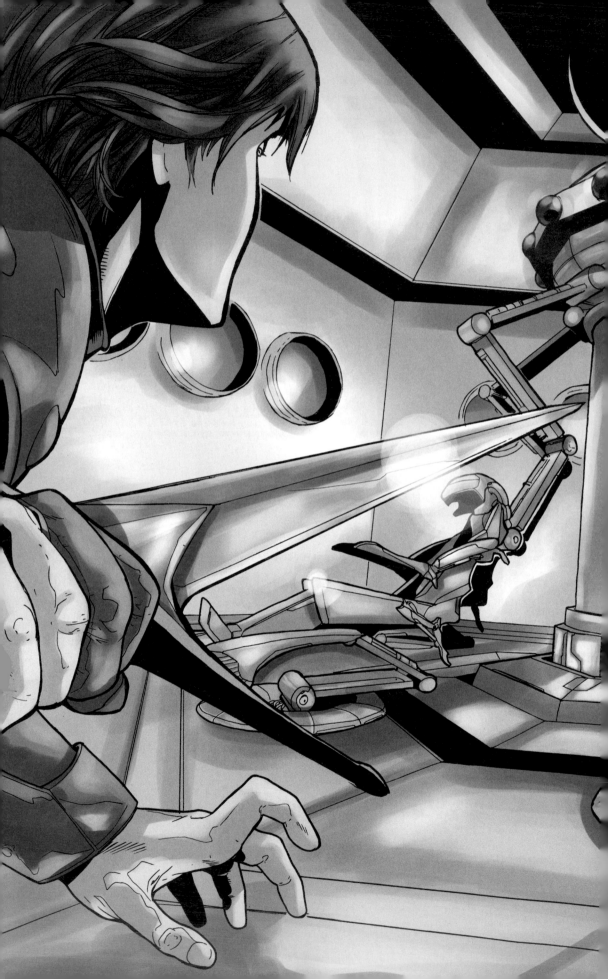

I'M COMING, BILLOS --

-- MY LOVE.

YOU AREN'T SUPPOSED TO BE HERE.

BUT THEN --

-- YOU HUMANS ALWAYS DO SEEM TO LOSE YOUR WAY.

ARE YOU HUNTER, THE ONE NAMED AFTER OUR COMMANDER?

WHO'S NAMED AFTER WHO, I ALWAYS SAY.

BUT YES, I AM HUNTER. AND YOU'RE DARSAL, ONE OF THE CHOSEN ONES.

AMAZING. MY HORSE DIDN'T EVEN FLINCH WHEN YOU LANDED. DOES IT KNOW YOU'RE THERE?

OF COURSE IT DOES.

HOWEVER, WE ROUSH ARE ENEMIES OF NO ONE BUT SHATAIKI.

IT COULD EVEN SLEEP LIKE A CHICK WITH ME PERCHED ON ITS HEAD.

REALLY?

SURE! I'LL SHOW YOU.

SEE? NO PROBLEMO.

JUST GOTTA KEEP YOUR BALANCE AND --

-- TA DA!

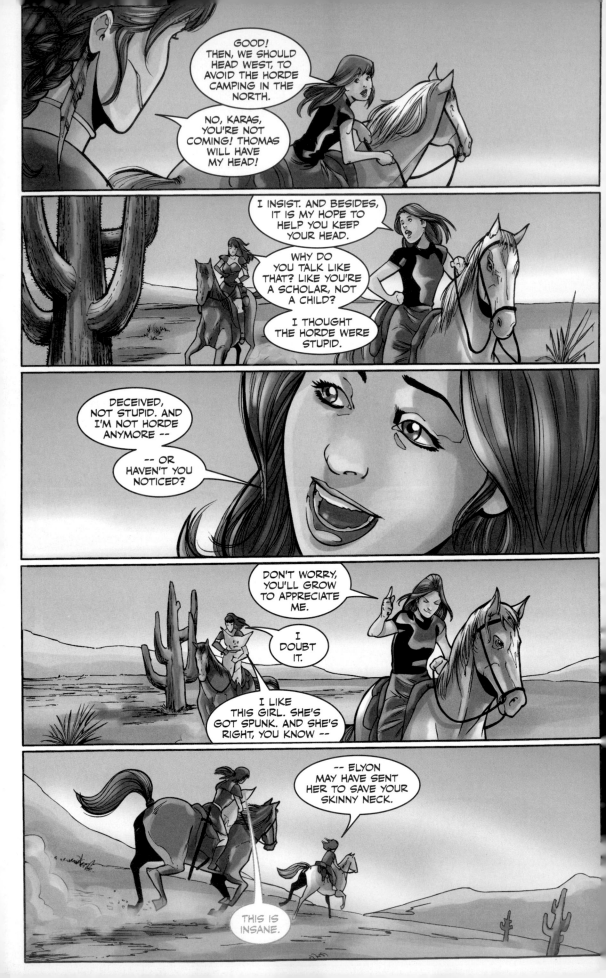

YOU WANT ME TO FLY?! I TOLD YOU, YOU NEED SLEEP.

NOT YOU, SQUAT. I WAS TALKING TO HUNTER.

THE COMMANDER?

NO, THE ROUSH! HE'S BEEN SITTING ON MY HORSE THE WHOLE TIME.

NOW, IF YOU DON'T MIND --

FINE, FINE, I'M GOING! BUT I DON'T LIKE IT.

I SUPPOSE THE LEAST I CAN DO IS GIVE YOU TWO SETS OF EYES.

FOR THIS INNOCENT ONE --

-- WHO HAS EARS TO HEAR AND EYES TO SEE --

-- LET HER HEAR AND SEE.

OH!

*—SEE THE *INFIDEL* GRAPHIC NOVEL.

LOOK, MAYBE YOU ARE MY NIECE. IF SO, I HAVE AN OBLIGATION TO PROTECT YOU.

HUNTER THE ROUSH KNOWS YOU'RE OUT HERE AND JOHNIS IS PROBABLY ALREADY ON HIS WAY.

DOESN'T THAT SOUND LIKE THE SAFEST PLAN?

KARAS?

EASY NOW OR THE LITTLE ONE LOSES HER VOICE.

THAT'S IT. COME TO PAPA.

MAYBE JOHNIS AND I SHOULD LEAVE ALONE TO LOOK FOR THEM.

AND JUST WHERE WOULD YOU BEGIN?

DO YOU HAVE SOME INTELLIGENCE THAT I'M NOT AWARE OF?

WITH ALL DUE RESPECT, SIR, THAT'S OUR PROBLEM.

AND YOU'RE MY PROBLEM.

I'M BEGINNING TO WONDER IF ELYON'S PURPOSE IN CHOOSING YOU WAS TO MORTIFY ME.

OH, JUST LET THEM GO ALREADY.

THAT SAID, I SUPPOSE I HAVE NO CHOICE BUT TO TRUST YOU INTO HIS CARE AND SEND YOU AFTER THE OTHERS.

I CERTAINLY CAN'T RISK THE LIVES OF MORE GUARD ON SUCH A RECKLESS ENDEAVOR.

COME ALONG NOW, WE HAVE TO HURRY!

WATER AND SWORDS. LOTS OF WATER!

THANK YOU SO MUCH, COMMANDER.

YES, YES. NOW, GET MOVING. THE SUN DOESN'T STOP --

-- NOT EVEN FOR THE CHOSEN ONE.

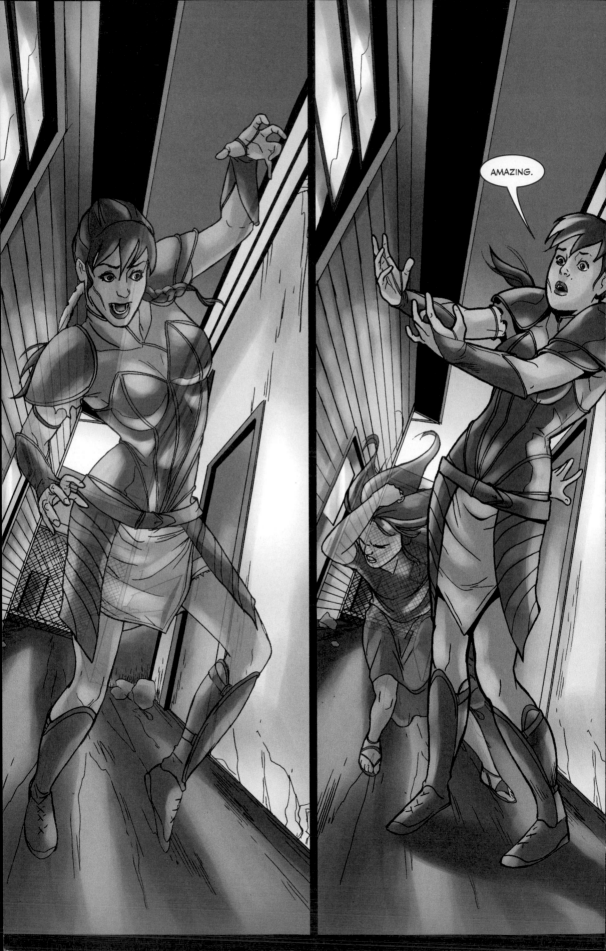

REMEMBER, YOU HAVE TO USE ELYON'S WATER. THEY'RE TERRIFIED OF THE WATER.

WE KNOW.

AND I CAN'T GO. NOT WITHOUT BACKUP.

THOSE NASTY VERMIN WILL RIP MY WINGS OFF AND FEED THEM TO THEIR YOUNG. WE CAN'T HAVE ANY YOUNG SHATAIKI GROWING UP WITH ROUSH IN THEIR BELLIES.

SO WE'VE BEEN TOLD.

SPEAKING OF YOUR LONG-LOST *FRIENDS*, ISN'T THAT THEM?

WHAT? OH MY, WHERE?

OKAY, OKAY. THAT'S THEM, THAT'S THEM.

AND DON'T THINK THEY DON'T LEARN.

YOU LOSE YOUR WATER AND YOU'RE DEAD MEAT --

-- AS THOMAS LIKES TO SAY.

I, FOR ONE, HAVE NEVER BEEN PARTICULARLY FOND OF THAT SAYING --

" -- REGARDLESS OF HOW APPROPRIATE IT MIGHT BE."

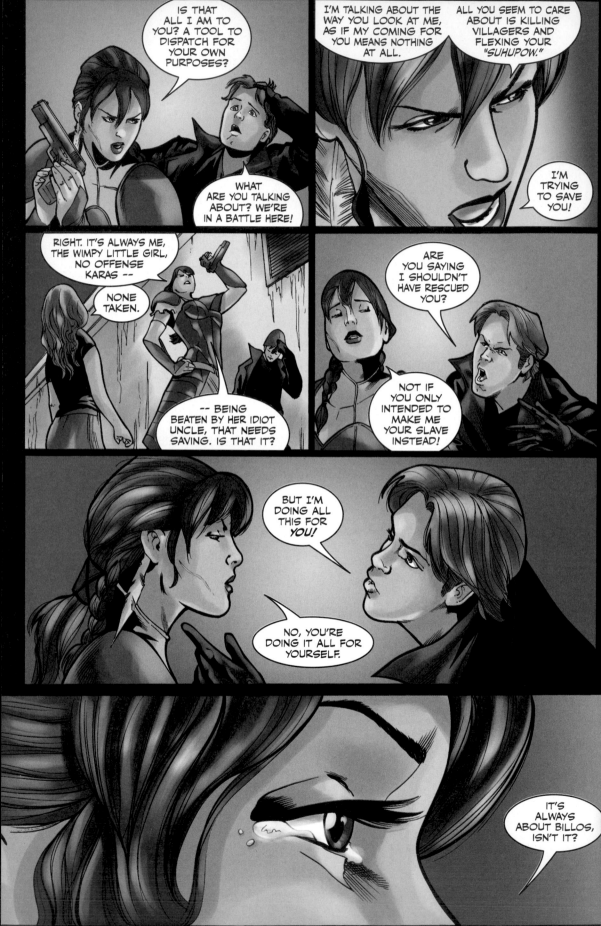

SNAP

WE'RE ALMOST THERE.

HOW CAN YOU TELL?

IT'S ALMOST IDENTICAL TO TEELEH'S LAIR*.

*-SEE THE *CHOSEN* GRAPHIC NOVEL.

SORRY I MISSED IT.

ME TOO.

AND WHAT ARE WE LOOKING FOR?

I MEAN, ASIDE FROM KARAS AND DARSAL.

ALUCARD'S CHAMBERS.

THERE *IS A WAY, YOU KNOW.*

WHAT ARE YOU TALKING ABOUT?

THERE'S HUNDREDS OF THEM, I'M INJURED AND I DON'T EVEN HAVE A WEAPON!

DARSAL'S AS GOOD AS DEAD.

I MEANT FOR YOU.

YOU NEED A WAY MORE THAN SHE DOES.

HOW CAN YOU SAY THAT?!

BLACK HAS HER!

NO, BILLOS --

-- BLACK HAS YOU.

FOLLOW ME, BILLOS.

COME --

-- AND I'LL GIVE YOU SOME-THING THAT MAKES *SUHUPOW* LOOK SILLY.

OKAY.

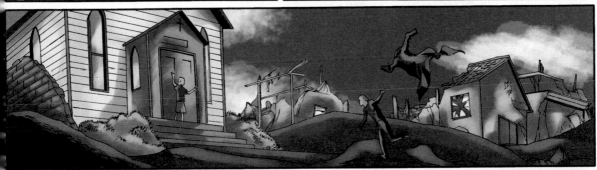

DIVE DEEP, BILLOS.

DIVE DEEP.

WRITTEN BY TED DEKKER
ADAPTATION BY J.S. EARLS AND KEVIN KAISER
EDITED BY KEVIN KAISER AND JOCELYN BAILEY
ILLUSTRATIONS BY EDUARDO PANSICA
COLORS BY ALE STARLING
LETTERED BY ZACH MATHENY
FRONT COVER ART BY RICARDO RATTON

© 2009 BY THOMAS NELSON PUBLISHERS

PUBLISHED IN NASHVILLE, TENNESSEE, BY THOMAS NELSON. THOMAS NELSON IS A REGISTERED TRADEMARK OF THOMAS NELSON, INC.

THOMAS NELSON, INC. TITLES MAY BE PURCHASED IN BULK FOR EDUCATIONAL, BUSINESS, FUND-RAISING, OR SALES PROMOTIONAL USE. FOR INFORMATION, PLEASE E-MAIL SPECIALMARKETS@THOMASNELSON.COM.

Library of Congress Cataloging in Publication Data

Earls, J. S.
    Renegade / story by Ted Dekker ; adapted by J.S. Earls and Kevin Kaiser.
      p. cm. — (The lost books ; 3)
    Summary: Relates, in graphic novel format, that as Johnis, Silvie, Billos, and Darsal continue their quest for the four still missing Books of History, Billos makes a decision that has devastating consequences for himself and his companions, especially the devoted Darsal.
    ISBN 978-1-59554-605-0 (softcover)
    1. Graphic novels. [1. Graphic novels. 2. Fantasy. 3. Christian life—Fiction.] I. Kaiser, Kevin. II. Dekker, Ted, 1962– III. Title.
PZ7.7.E17Ren 2009
741.5'973—dc22   2008053423

Printed in Canada
09 10 11 12 13 QW 5 4 3 2 1

Two Realities. One Experience.
Seven Graphic Novels.

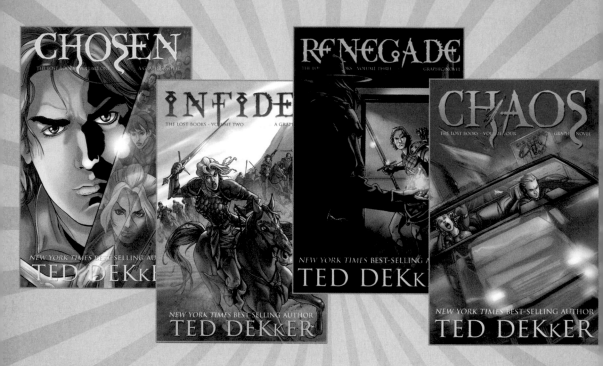

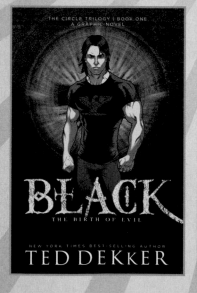

THE BEGINNING . . . AND THE END ARE NEAR

NEW YORK TIMES BEST-SELLING AUTHOR

TED DEKkER

GREEN

THE CIRCLE | BOOK ZERO   THE BEGINNING AND THE END

BOOK ZERO ARRIVES
SEPTEMBER 1, 2009

THE LOST BOOKS
THE MAKING OF THE GRAPHIC NOVELS

At Thomas Nelson we are passionate about storytelling and enjoy the thrill of introducing exciting new authors to readers for the first time. But we are equally passionate about surprising our best-selling authors' fans by retelling their favorite tales in fresh ways.

Joining us for a behind-the-scenes look at one way we are doing that is Kevin Kaiser, a writer and Editor in Chief of the Lost Books graphic novels, which are based on Ted Dekker's best-selling young adult novels.

Thomas Nelson: Thanks for joining us, Kevin. What exactly is a graphic novel?

Kevin Kaiser: It's really just a long-form comic book. Imagine taking your favorite novel and seeing the heroes, villains, and the world they occupy come to life visually. That's what a graphic novel is: an illustrated story. In a way, it's words becoming flesh.

TN: Describe the Lost Books graphic novels. How is the story different from the books?

KK: When storytelling is involved, it's tough to beat Dekker, so the story in the graphic novels unfolds as it does in the books. But we did wrap it in a slightly different skin. We adapted each book (about 260 pages) into four, 132-page comic books. Fans will notice immediately that the story is compressed, so the pacing is much faster—if you can imagine that with a Dekker story.

TN: What kind of quality would comic fans find if they picked up these books?

KK: Well done is better than well said, so I'll let these books speak for themselves. I will say this much: most of our production team has worked for DC Comics, Marvel, and other top-tier publishers in the business. They aren't wannabe artists; they are world-class professionals. To see what I mean fans should pick up the Circle Trilogy graphic novels or visit **www.thecircletrilogy.com** to see some of their previous work.

TN: You mentioned the Circle Trilogy graphic novels, which you also produced. Tell us about the process. How does a novel become a graphic novel?

KK: It's a very involved process that takes about a year from concept to shelf. In many ways, adapting a novel into a visual format is similar to filmmaking. In fact, some of the most popular films in past years were graphic novels first. Let me walk you through the process.

CASTING CALL

KK: Several things happen at once, but we generally begin with concept art. First, we go through the book, make a descriptive profile for each character, and ask lots of questions. What color is this character's hair? How tall is he? What kind of clothes does he wear? We then work with the artists to flesh out (literally!) what each character should look like. It involves input from a team of people, including Ted himself, engaging in lively discussion.

Think about the last time you read a book. Did you have a fully formed image in your mind's eye of what a character looked like? You probably did, but maybe not as detailed as you think. Generality is not a luxury we have. Not only do we have to capture a character's appearance in detail, but also their personality and mannerisms. You only get one chance to design characters and the world they live in, so we want to get it right. Add on top of that, several people are involved in the process, and each of them has different ideas of what a character should and shouldn't be. It involves a lot of trial and error.

Below are two options for what Billos would look like. We ultimately chose the one on the left.

THE SCRIPT

KK: Next is writing the script. Just as every film needs a screenplay for the director and actors to follow, our artists need a script so they know how to draw a particular page.

The process begins with our writing team, led by the talented JS (Jeff) Earls, dividing each book into distinct "acts" and then outlining the book chapter by chapter, noting the main "beats" of the story. We then work through where the story can be streamlined, where it can't, and what story elements we could deliver in other ways. Remember, we only have 132 pages to tell the same story Ted told in 260, so brevity is essential. To give you context, that equals about 250 words per page in the novel, but only about 30-50 per graphic novel page.

Each graphic novel page is then written in screenplay format, then ruthlessly edited and rewritten until it's right. The end result is a "road map" of narrative (what's happening) and dialogue (what the characters are saying) to guide the artists in the next step.

Below is an example of a scripted scene from Chosen

CHOSEN, Page 9, Adapted by JS Earls

Panel 1 - Very dramatic two-shot of the Red team's Silvie (in front) and Jackov (close behind) running toward (us) the bouncing Horde Ball!

JACKOV
Grab the ball, Silvie. I'll take care of Billos.

SILVIE
I'm on it.

Panel 2 - Silhouette long shot of Silvie leaping high into the air (above the mound), reaching her arms out, her fingers almost touching the ball. On the ground, behind her - Jackov rushes forward. On the ground, in front of her - Billos approaches with Darsal close behind.

Panel 3 - Close-up of Silvie's hands grabbing the Horde Ball.

Panel 4 - Action shot of Silvie, hunched over (like a "cannonball"), cradling the ball in her gut as she rolls in the air. Below her, Billos reaches up for Silvie, but she is out of his reach.

SILVIE 2
Now, Jackov!

Panel 5 - Violent view of Jackov diving into Billos, tackling him hard enough to knock the wind out of Billos and lift his feet from the ground!

BILLOS (LOUD)
OoOof!

ROUGH LAYOUT

KK: Next up is layout, when the storytelling baton is passed from the writer/adapters to the artist. The lead artist takes the script and translates the written word into action for the first time. Like a cinematographer, his job is to breathe life into a scene through camera angles, perspective, and scene flow. Significant thought is invested into layouts, and we explore several combinations of panel size, type and arrangement until we find just the right look and feel for a page. Below is an artist's rendering of the script on the previous page.

You'll notice that the art is not very refined. That's intentional. A layout is just the artist's rough draft of a page, and it gives us the chance to tweak different elements of a scene quickly. That even includes ensuring there is room for the speech bubbles. Notice the numbered captions, which are tied to dialogue from the script. Only after we have settled on an overall feel that is right will the artist draw the final art.

FINAL ART AND INKS

KK: After the layout is finalized, the artist draws the page in detail. This is the first time the page begins to look like it will in the book, though it is certainly far from complete. After it is drawn, the page then goes through a rigorous editorial process to ensure the visual story is sharp. We look at *every* detail, including things like making sure a character's shadow falls in the right place given the angle of the lighting in the panel. Every detail is important. But again, it takes time. On average, each page takes a full working day to draw, not including any revisions that will need to be made during the editorial process.

Here is the next phase of the same scene depicted on the previous page

COLORING AND LETTERING

KK: After everything is drawn and finalized, everything goes to another team of artists who specialize in digital coloring. From there, each page then goes to a letterer who inserts all of the speech bubbles, sound effects and captions. And, you have a graphic novel. Of course, there's all of the post-production work, assembly, printing, and manufacturing left to be done. But, we'll save that conversation for another day. (Laughs.)

Scene with lettering and sound effects

THE LOST BOOKS

THE BOOKS THAT INSPIRED THE GRAPHIC NOVELS